A TEMPLAR BOOK

Produced by The Templar Company plc,
Pippbrook Mill, London Road, Dorking, Surrey RH4 1JE, Great Britain.

This edition produced for Parragon Books,
Unit 13-17, Avonbridge Trading Estate, Atlantic Road, Avonmouth, Bristol BS11 9Q

This book contains material first published as
The Palace of Bricks in Enid Blyton's Sunny Stories
and Sunny Stories between 1926 and 1953.

Illustrated by Pamela Venus

Printed and bound in Italy

ISBN 1 85813 518 4

Enid Blyton's

POCKET LIBRARY

THE TOYS' NEW PALACE

Illustrated by Pamela Venus

PARRAGON

Jack and Tilly had built a palace
with their bricks. It was a very
good one – very tall and grand,
with windows and a door and
lots of towers and turrets.
The children were
pleased with it.

BRICKS

"It's a pity nobody ever lives in the houses and palaces we build," said Tilly. "They are just wasted, really. We build them, and then we knock them down."

"I wish we didn't have to knock *this* palace down," said Jack, looking at it proudly. "It really is one of the best we've ever made, don't you think? Look, Mummy! Don't you think our palace is good?"

"Splendid!" said Mummy. "But now it's time for bed so you must put your bricks away."

"Couldn't we leave this palace up for just one night?" said Tilly longingly. "It's such a fine palace after all and it has taken us all day to build. It would be so nice to lie in bed and think of it standing here in the moonlight, looking so real."

"We could imagine that the fairies had arrived and were having a grand feast inside it," added Jack. "Wouldn't that be fun!"

"Well, you can leave it till the morning if you want to," said Mummy. "But, now, you must hurry off to bed. It's past your bedtime already."

Little did the children realise that, as soon as they had left the room, their toys all started to come to life. The big teddy bear let all the toys out of the toy cupboard. The dolls woke up inside the doll's house. All the animals on the toy farm came awake and the clockwork train started running about all over the floor.

It happened every night and this night the toys were pleased to find that the children had left them a splendid palace to play in. They thought it was a very fine present indeed!

When the children were safely in bed, and the nursery was in darkness except for the big silver moon shining through the window, the big teddy bear ran right across the nursery floor and looked through the doorway of the fine wooden palace.

"I say! It's the best thing that ever was!" he called. "Come on toys! Look what the children have built for us! See this window – and that one – and look at the turrets and spires at the top. My, haven't they built it well!"

"It's splendid," said one of the dolls' house dolls. "Can we go inside?"

Just then there came a loud banging noise from just above them. It was someone knocking on the nursery window.

"Come in!" called the teddy bear, surprised that anyone could come calling so late at night. And he was even more astonished when a large grey mouse appeared on the windowsill wearing a postman's cap on his head. He carried a letter in his hand and was busy looking all around the nursery for someone particular to deliver it to.

"Does the clockwork mouse live here?" he asked.

"Oh yes!" squeaked the little mouse in astonishment, and he ran over to the postman. "Here I am!"

"I have a letter for you from the King of Mice," said the postman in an important voice, handing it over.

Then
he turned
on his tail and
was gone again. The
toys heard him pattering
away along the garden path.
The clockwork mouse stared at his
letter in surprise. Then he tore it open.

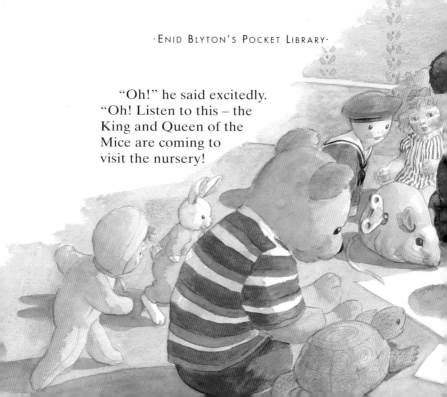

"Oh!" he said excitedly. "Oh! Listen to this – the King and Queen of the Mice are coming to visit the nursery!

They are on their way to Mouseland,
and they have decided to stay here
for the night! They ask if they can
be my guests! Oh, what an
honour it is to be sure!"

The clockwork mouse was so excited that he ran up and down the nursery without stopping. Up and down and up and down he went, until his clockwork ran down. and the teddy had to wind him up again.

"There is only one problem," said the mouse when he had calmed down. "The toy cupboard is all very well, but it would be so much nicer if I had a special place where the King and Queen could stay. I've only my old box for them to sleep in, and nothing at all to offer them to eat. Oh dear, I wish I could think of something better! What shall I do?

Fancy the King and Queen coming to stay here! I can't get over the surprise!"

"Don't worry Clockwork Mouse," said the big teddy bear , patting him on the back. "I have just had a wonderful idea. We can give the King and Queen of the Mice a splendid welcome. They can spend the night in a palace – the palace of bricks! It's just the right size for them! And as a special treat I will hide behind the coal scuttle with the musical box and turn the handle so that it plays music for them when they arrive."

"And I know where Jack dropped half his biscuit this morning," said the curly-haired doll excitedly. "It rolled into the corner of the floor over there!"

"And there are two sweets left in the toy sweet shop. I saw them there this afternoon!" said Panda. "Oh, Clockwork Mouse, you don't need to be worried – we will help you to welcome the King and Queen of the Mice. They are sure to have a lovely time!"

Well, you should have seen how those toys rushed about to get things ready!

First, they took all the furniture and the tiny rugs from the old dolls' house and put them into the palace of bricks. They found blankets and pillows for the tiny beds to make them comfortable. Then two of the rag dolls leaned out of the big nursery window and picked some flowers to put on the table.

The teddy bear found a little toy lantern and managed to hang it from the ceiling of the palace. He switched it on. How lovely the palace of bricks looked with the light shining inside!

The curly-haired doll found the bit of biscuit and put it on a tiny plate on the table. Meanwhile Panda and the toy dog carried the sweet bottle out of the toy shop and arranged the sweets on the table too. Just then there was a shout from Clockwork Mouse. He had found half a cup of lemonade that the children had left. It would make a fine drink for the King and Queen.

Then the teddy bear hid the musical box behind the coal scuttle. He began to turn the handle! The music sounded so lovely – everything was ready!

Just then, out from a hole in the floor
boards came the King and Queen of the
Mice! They had tiny crowns on their heads,
and looked rather funny – but, dear me,
they were the King and Queen all right!
Twenty small mice followed them, blowing
on twenty golden trumpets as they came.

The clockwork mouse, with a new blue bow round his neck, ran to welcome them all. Then he proudly lead them to the palace of bricks, bowing politely. The King and Queen were amazed and delighted.

"What a fine place you have here, Clockwork Mouse!" said the King. "And what lovely music!" said the Queen, looking all round for the band. But of course she didn't see the teddy bear hiding behind the coal scuttle, turning the musical box handle as fast as he could!

"And you've provided a feast too!" said the King, beginning to nibble the biscuit. "Very nice, Clockwork Mouse, very nice indeed."

"Look at these lovely sweets!" said the Queen Mouse, tasting one. "This surely must be one of the nicest places we have ever visited. It is most kind of you, little mouse."

After they had eaten, the King and Queen had a fine dance all around the palace and invited the toys to join in. Soon the whole nursery was filled with dancing figures and the poor teddy bear played the musical box till his arm nearly fell off.

In the middle of it all Jack and Tilly
heard the musical box playing and came to
see what was going on! How they stared
when they saw what was going on!

Their palace of bricks shone like gold in
the light of the toy lantern. And all over the
nursery floor there were toys and mice
playing and dancing to the sound of sweet
music.

But as soon as the toys saw the two
children they scampered inside the palace
and hid, and Jack and Tilly thought they
must have imagined the whole thing.

Anyway, the first light of morning
was beginning to shine through
the nursery window. It was
time for the King and
Queen to leave for
Mouseland.

"Goodbye, Clockwork Mouse! Goodbye, toys!"
they squeaked, as they disappeared through
the hole in the floorboards.
"We'll send you an invitation to our palace
one day!" they said and the next
minute they had gone.

Later that morning the children came to play in the nursery. The palace of bricks looked quite ordinary in the daylight and Jack and Tilly were disappointed to think that what they had seen had been nothing but a dream.

But can you guess what happened? Why, the toys had forgotten to take out the chairs and tables and lanterns.

"Goodness me!" exclaimed Jack. "So we did see something after all!"

"We wanted someone to live in our palace, and they did!" said Tilly, in delight.

As for the clockwork mouse, he is very happy now, for any day he is expecting an invitation from the King of the Mice to go and stay with him at *his* palace in Mouseland. I hope it comes soon, don't you?